DINOSAURS
Everywhere!

by Carol Harrison

Illustrated by Richard Courtney

Cartwheel
·B·O·O·K·S·®

SCHOLASTIC INC.

New York   Toronto   London   Auckland   Sydney
Mexico City   New Delhi   Hong Kong   Buenos Aires

P9-DCV-599

For William
— C.H.

For Adrienne and Bethany Courtney
— R.C.

Consultant:
Robert Asher, D.P.A.S.
State University of New York, Stony Brook

Author's Note:
Throughout this book, all the dinosaurs shown interacting with each other
lived in roughly the same time and place. Some of the dinosaurs pictured in the
large scenes on the cover and on pages 6, 16, and 32, however, lived in the
same time period, but their fossils were not necessarily found in the same area.

Text copyright © 1998 by Carol Harrison.
Illustrations copyright © 1998 by Richard Courtney.
All rights reserved. Published by Scholastic Inc.
CARTWHEEL BOOKS and the CARTWHEEL BOOKS logo
are trademarks and/or registered trademarks of Scholastic Inc.

No part of this publication may be reproduced, or stored in a retrieval system, or transmitted in any form or by
any means, electronic, mechanical, photocopying, recording, or otherwise, without written permission of the
publisher. For information regarding permissions, write to Scholastic Inc., Attention: Permissions Department,
557 Broadway, New York, NY 10012.

Library of Congress Cataloging-in-Publication Data
Harrison, Carol, 1953-
        Dinosaurs everywhere! / by Carol Harrison : illustrated by Richard Courtney.
            p.   cm.
        Summary: Discusses the probable structure and behavior of dinosaurs and describes such
    individual species as the Tyrannosaurus, Maiasaura, and Seismosaurus.
            ISBN 0-590-00089-6
        1. Dinosaurs — Juvenile literature.   [1. Dinosaurs.]
        I. Courtney, Richard, 1955-   ill.   II. Title.
        QE862.D5H264   1998
    567.9— dc21   97-44640
                                                                                    CIP
                                                                                     AC

20 19 18 17 16 15 14 13 12   08 09 10

Printed in Singapore   46
First printing, November 1998

CONTENTS

Dinosaurs Everywhere   6

Dinosaurs Big and Small   8

Dinosaur Fossils   10

On a Dinosaur Dig   12

Dinosaur Skeletons   14

Dinosaur Dinners   16

Plant-Eaters   18

Meat-Eaters   19

Fighting and Biting   20

Dinosaur Defenses   22

Fossil Footprints   24

Tales Tracks Tell   26

Baby Dinosaurs   28

Dinosaur Families   30

Other Animals from Dinosaur Days   32

In a Dinosaur Museum   34

Dinosaurs on Display   36

Good-Bye, Dinosaurs   38

DINOSAURS EVERYWHERE

A long, long, *long* time ago, before there were any people, dinosaurs lived on the earth. In those days, there were no houses or roads anywhere. But there were trees and ferns, rocks and oceans, deserts and rain forests.

TYRANNOSAURUS
(ty-RAN-uh-sawr-us)

MAIASAURA
(mah-ee-ah-SAWR-ah)

Much of the world was warmer than it is today, and dinosaurs lived just about everywhere. Dinosaurs lived in the forests and on the plains. Dinosaurs lived in muddy swamps and in sandy deserts.

NEMEGTOSAURUS
(NEH-meg-tuh-sawr-us)

OVIRAPTOR
(oh-vih-RAP-tor)

7

DINOSAURS BIG AND SMALL

TYRANNOSAURUS

Tyrannosaurus was the biggest dinosaur that had sharp teeth and claws. Its head was so big, you could have climbed right into its mouth! Tyrannosaurus stood on two legs. It probably used its short arms to push itself up off the ground.

MAIASAURA

Maiasaura could stand on all four legs, but it ran on two. Was it fast enough to get away from Tyrannosaurus? Probably not, when Tyrannosaurus was this close.

COMPSOGNATHUS
(komp-so-NAY-thus)

Compsognathus was one of the smallest dinosaurs. It would have fit easily into a grocery bag. It weighed less than a big jar of peanut butter. Compsognathus had hands with two fingers that could reach out and catch lizards and other small animals.

8

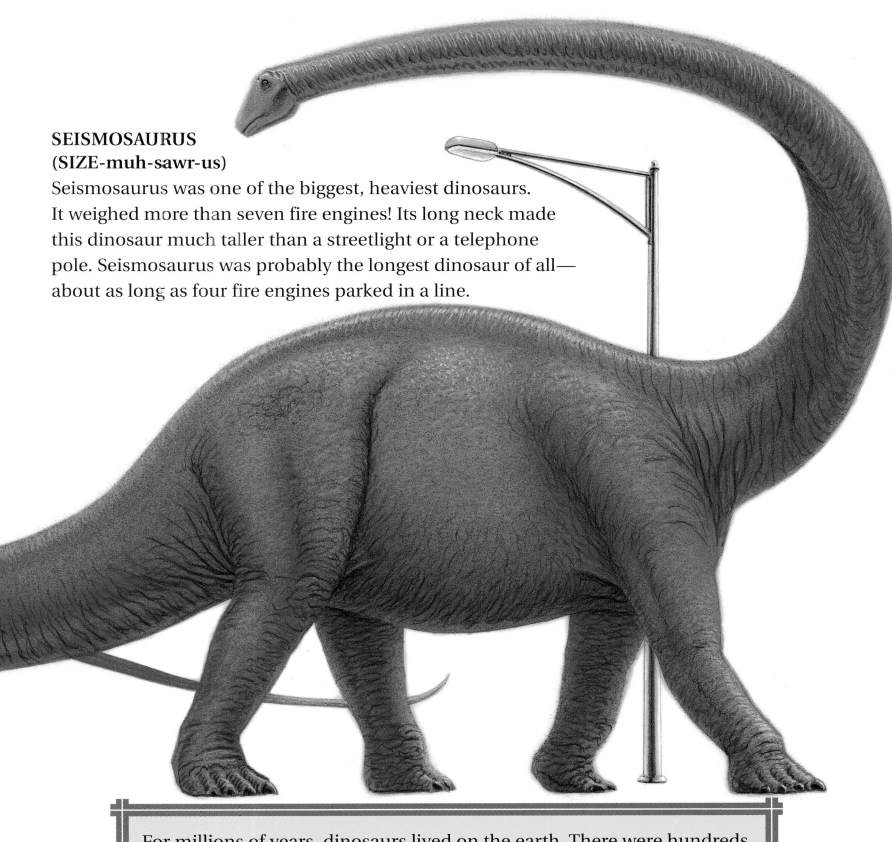

SEISMOSAURUS
(SIZE-muh-sawr-us)

Seismosaurus was one of the biggest, heaviest dinosaurs. It weighed more than seven fire engines! Its long neck made this dinosaur much taller than a streetlight or a telephone pole. Seismosaurus was probably the longest dinosaur of all— about as long as four fire engines parked in a line.

For millions of years, dinosaurs lived on the earth. There were hundreds of different kinds of dinosaurs, but not all of them lived at the very same time. Compsognathus and Seismosaurus actually died out millions of years before Tyrannosaurus and Maiasaura came along.

DINOSAUR FOSSILS

Under every dinosaur's skin was a skeleton made of bones.
(Most animals and all people have skeletons.) When a
dinosaur died, its skin dried up and crumbled into dust.
All that was left was the skeleton.

Sometimes a dinosaur skeleton was covered up when the wind blew sand or a river washed mud over the bones. The bones lay in the ground for millions of years and slowly turned into stone. These rocklike bones are called *fossils*. Almost everything we know about dinosaurs we have learned from fossil bones.

ON A DINOSAUR DIG

"Dinosaur hunters" look for dinosaur fossils. The best places to find fossil bones are in a desert or in dry, rocky areas. Sometimes bones are found sticking right out of the ground! The dinosaur hunters dig up the bones very carefully so they won't break. There may be just a few bones, or there may be enough bones to put together to make a skeleton. Usually the bones are jumbled up and have to be put in the right places. Then everyone can see what the dinosaur looked like.

Another word for "dinosaur hunter" is *paleontologist* (PAY-lee-ahn-TAHL-uh-jist). Paleontologists are people who study fossils to learn about animals and plants that lived long, long ago. Dinosaur fossils give clues to paleontologists about what a dinosaur ate, how fast it could run, and other things.

DINOSAUR SKELETONS

This skeleton is so big that it must have come from a very heavy dinosaur. By studying the skeleton, paleontologists have figured out that Seismosaurus probably weighed as much as fifteen elephants. It must have shaken the ground when it walked. That's why the person who first discovered the skeleton named this dinosaur Seismosaurus, which means "earthquake lizard."

Paleontologists can tell that this small dinosaur was a fast runner. Its skeleton has long, thin legs and very lightweight, hollow bones, like birds have. The dinosaur was named Coelophysis (see-lo-FY-sis), which means "hollow form."

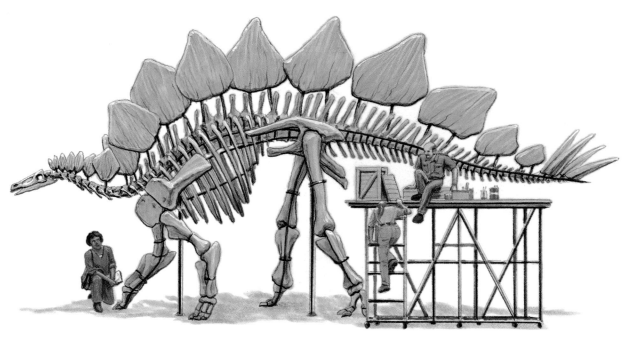

The big, heavy bones of this skeleton show paleontologists a dinosaur that must have moved slowly. This animal had many large plates on its back. That's why it was named Stegosaurus (STEG-uh-sawr-us), which means "plated lizard."

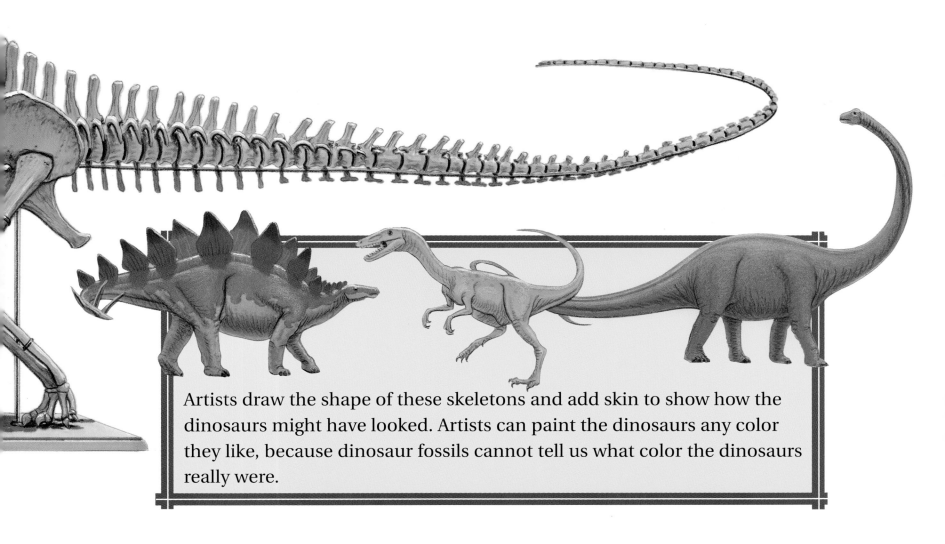

Artists draw the shape of these skeletons and add skin to show how the dinosaurs might have looked. Artists can paint the dinosaurs any color they like, because dinosaur fossils cannot tell us what color the dinosaurs really were.

DINOSAUR DINNERS

Paleontologists look at a dinosaur's teeth to find out what it ate. Some dinosaurs had sharp, pointed teeth. Those knife-like teeth were just right for taking bites out of other animals. Dinosaurs that ate animals are called meat-eaters.

Most dinosaurs ate plants. Their teeth were not pointed. Different plant-eaters had different kinds of teeth. Flat teeth were good for chewing up leaves. Longer teeth, shaped like unsharpened pencils, were good for biting off leaves and branches.

VELOCIRAPTOR
(veh-loss-ih-RAP-tor)

PROTOCERATOPS
(pro-toe-SAIR-uh-tops)

TITANOSAURUS
(TY-tan-uh-sawr-us)

EDMONTOSAURUS
(ed-MON-tuh-sawr-us)

TRICERATOPS
(try-SAIR-uh-tops)

PLANT-EATERS

DIPLODOCUS (dih-PLOD-uh-kus) used its pencil-shaped teeth to rake pine needles from a large branch into its mouth. This dinosaur swallowed its food without chewing. It also swallowed stones! They stayed in the dinosaur's stomach and helped mash up the plants that Diplodocus ate. Big dinosaurs like this one needed so much food that they probably spent most of their time eating.

TRICERATOPS had a strong, sharp beak that helped it bite off thick stems and branches. With its short, flat teeth, Triceratops could chew up tough plants that other dinosaurs couldn't eat.

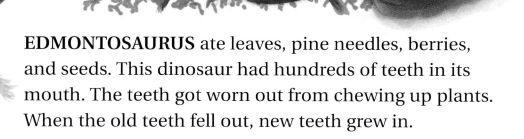

EDMONTOSAURUS ate leaves, pine needles, berries, and seeds. This dinosaur had hundreds of teeth in its mouth. The teeth got worn out from chewing up plants. When the old teeth fell out, new teeth grew in.

MEAT-EATERS

HERRERASAURUS (eh-RAY-rah-sawr-us) was one of the first dinosaurs. It had sharp teeth—perfect for eating other animals.

OVIRAPTOR didn't have any teeth. It used its hard beak to eat insects and little animals like lizards. Oviraptor and other small meat-eaters also may have eaten eggs.

PROTOCERATOPS

VELOCIRAPTOR ate other dinosaurs. It ran fast enough to catch small dinosaurs and hold them with its claws.

19

FIGHTING AND BITING

Dinosaurs fought with each other, just as other animals sometimes do. Male dinosaurs fought to get female partners. Some dinosaurs fought to keep others out of their territory. Plant-eaters fought to protect themselves from meat-eaters.

Ankylosaurus could hit an attacker with the bony club on the end of its tail. Dinosaurs with horns, such as Anchiceratops and Styracosaurus, would charge at each other and crash their horns together when they fought. *Ouch!*

STYRACOSAURUS
(sty-RAK-uh-sawr-us)

ANCHICERATOPS
(ANG-kee-sair-uh-tops)

ANKYLOSAURUS
(ang-KYLE-uh-sawr-us)

DEINONYCHUS
(dyne-ON-ik-us)

21

DINOSAUR DEFENSES

PACHYCEPHALOSAURUS (pak-ee-SEF-ah-lo-sawr-us) had a hard, bony cap on top of its head. The cap was much thicker than a bike helmet. It didn't hurt this dinosaur to bash its head in a fight. Pachycephalosaurus fought its enemies by butting them away.

DEINONYCHUS

PARASAUROLOPHUS (par-ah-sawr-OL-uh-fus) had a long crest on top of its head. This was not a horn for fighting, but it may have been a horn for blowing. Parasaurolophus could probably honk or bellow loudly to warn its herd when danger was nearby.

**ALBERTOSAURUS
(al-BUR-tuh-sawr-us)**

22

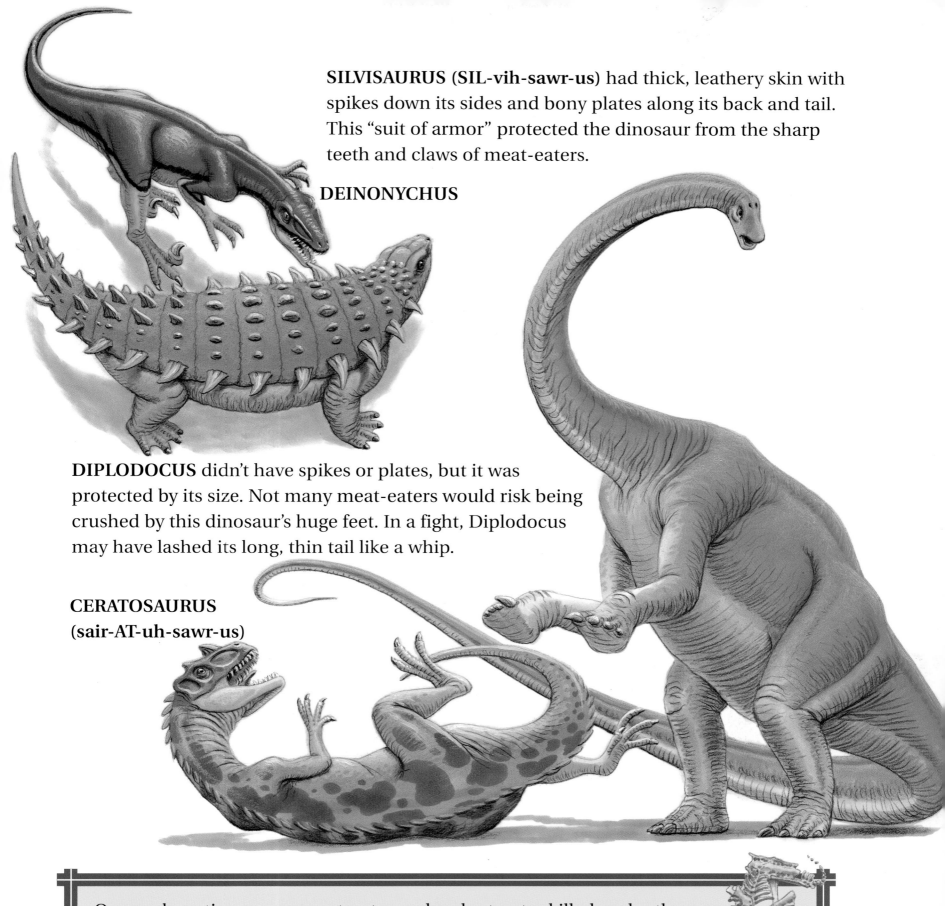

SILVISAURUS (SIL-vih-sawr-us) had thick, leathery skin with spikes down its sides and bony plates along its back and tail. This "suit of armor" protected the dinosaur from the sharp teeth and claws of meat-eaters.

DEINONYCHUS

DIPLODOCUS didn't have spikes or plates, but it was protected by its size. Not many meat-eaters would risk being crushed by this dinosaur's huge feet. In a fight, Diplodocus may have lashed its long, thin tail like a whip.

CERATOSAURUS
(sair-AT-uh-sawr-us)

Once, a long time ago, a meat-eater and a plant-eater killed each other in a fight. Their skeletons lay in the ground together and became fossils. Paleontologists discovered the bones and dug them up. The meat-eater was still holding onto the other dinosaur's head.

23

FOSSIL FOOTPRINTS

When dinosaurs walked on wet ground, they left footprints.
As the sun dried the ground, the footprints hardened.
Sometimes the footprints were buried by dirt or mud.
They lay in the ground for millions of years and became
rock-hard fossils.

Plant-eater footprints

BRACHIOSAURUS
(BRAK-ee-uh-sawr-us)

Paleontologists have found dinosaur footprints in rock all over the world. They study the rock to find out when the dinosaurs lived. They study the footprints to learn more about dinosaurs—especially how dinosaurs acted with each other.

ALLOSAURUS
(AL-uh-sawr-us)

Meat-eater footprints

25

TALES TRACKS TELL

A line of dinosaur footprints is called a *track*. Fossil tracks have often been found side by side. They show that more than one dinosaur was walking together. That's how paleontologists learned that some kinds of dinosaurs lived together in herds at least part of the time.

Plant-eater track

Paleontologists can tell whether a footprint was made by a meat-eater or a plant-eater by looking at the footprint's shape. These big, rounded footprints were made by a long-necked plant-eater, such as Brachiosaurus.

Inside this main track is a line of smaller footprints. They belonged to a baby. These little footprints show that the plant-eaters traveled with their babies in the middle of the herd so meat-eaters couldn't get to them.

This track was made by a big meat-eater, such as Allosaurus. Its footprints show three pointed toes. Some of these meat-eater footprints are right on top of the plant-eater tracks. Did the meat-eater step on the plant-eaters' tracks minutes after they were made, or days later? No one knows for sure. But it's possible that the meat-eater was following the plant-eaters on purpose. The meat-eater would have been too small to attack a herd of big plant-eaters by itself. It may have been looking for a plant-eater that was too young, too old, or too sick to win a fight.

Meat-eater track

Paleontologists tell how fast a dinosaur traveled by looking at its footprints. Footprints that are far apart show the dinosaur was running. Allosaurus could run almost as fast as a person.

BABY DINOSAURS

Dinosaur mothers laid their eggs in nests on the ground. Some kinds of dinosaurs took care of their eggs before the babies hatched. Maiasaura covered the eggs with leaves and grass to keep them warm. This dinosaur probably guarded the nest to keep egg-stealing lizards away.

Many dinosaurs from one herd often made their nests and laid their eggs together. Some herds returned to the same nesting area year after year.

MAIASAURA

When Maiasaura's babies were hatched, they probably couldn't stand up yet. Maiasaura brought leaves or berries to the nest until the babies could walk. Then Maiasaura led the babies out of the nest to find food. Maiasaura had to be careful not to step on the tiny babies. The babies were probably kept near the nest until they had grown bigger, to keep them from being stepped on by the rest of the herd.

An Apatosaurus (ah-PAT-uh-sawr-us) baby was also very tiny compared to its huge, long-necked parents. But it grew quickly. In just a few weeks, it grew from the size of your pillow to the size of your bed!

APATOSAURUS baby

Different kinds of dinosaurs laid eggs of different shapes and sizes. Oviraptor laid eggs the size of big potatoes. Other eggs were rounder and larger, about the size of small watermelons. These eggs may have belonged to the big, long-necked dinosaur, Hypselosaurus (HIP-sih-luh-sawr-us).

Paleontologists can't tell from fossils what color the eggs were. So artists who draw dinosaur eggs generally use the colors we see on eggs today.

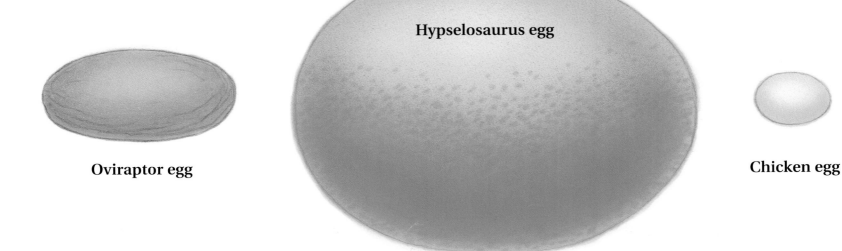

Hypselosaurus egg

Oviraptor egg

Chicken egg

DINOSAUR FAMILIES

Dinosaur babies that were big enough to leave the nesting area probably joined the herd. Fossil bones and footprints show there were herds of plant-eaters and herds of meat-eaters. A dinosaur herd was probably like a herd of cows or sheep—only one kind of dinosaur lived together in the herd.

TYRANNOSAURUS

This Triceratops herd is protecting its young dinosaurs. With horns longer than swords, Triceratops was probably able to scare away Tyrannosaurus.

TYRANNOSAURUS

TRICERATOPS

OTHER ANIMALS FROM DINOSAUR DAYS

Millions of years ago, the earth was full of animal life. Fish swam in the rivers. Turtles crawled on rocks warmed by the sun. Snakes slithered through the weeds. Frogs croaked at night. Small birds soared in the sky, along with other flying animals called pterosaurs (TAIR-uh-sawrz).

HYPSILOPHODON (hip-sih-LOHF-uh-don)

GALLIMIMUS (gal-ih-MY-mus)

BARYONYX
(bahr-ee-ON-iks)

Some small dinosaurs caught lizards or beetles to eat.
Crocodiles tried to catch the small dinosaurs. There were no
dogs or cats or horses in those days. There were no elephants
or tigers yet. The main land animals were dinosaurs.

IN A DINOSAUR MUSEUM

What do paleontologists do with a dinosaur skeleton when they have finished putting it together and studying it? They might want to put it on display in a museum for everyone to see. Some museums have real fossil skeletons. But most museums have plastic skeletons that are made to look exactly like the real ones.

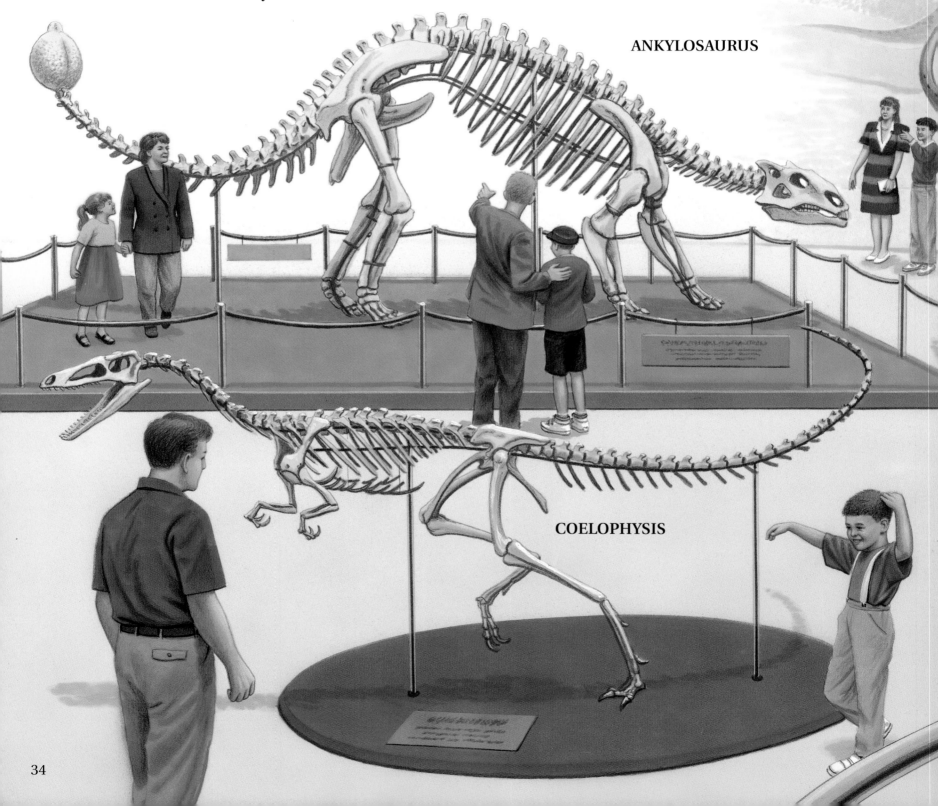

ANKYLOSAURUS

COELOPHYSIS

This museum has a model of Tyrannosaurus that moves and roars. But no one knows if Tyrannosaurus really roared. Fossils can't tell us what sounds dinosaurs made.

Model of TYRANNOSAURUS

Models of MUSSAURUS (moos-SAWR-us) babies

35

DINOSAURS ON DISPLAY

Some dinosaur museums have "hands-on" exhibits. Visitors can "dig up" skeletons, open plastic eggs, and handle all kinds of plastic dinosaur fossils. (The real fossils are too valuable to play with, and they would break too easily.) The plastic fossils are the same size as the real ones, but they are much lighter. A real horn from Triceratops would be too heavy to hold.

Tyrannosaurus teeth were nearly as long as your head.

A footprint made by Seismosaurus was about the size of a snow saucer!

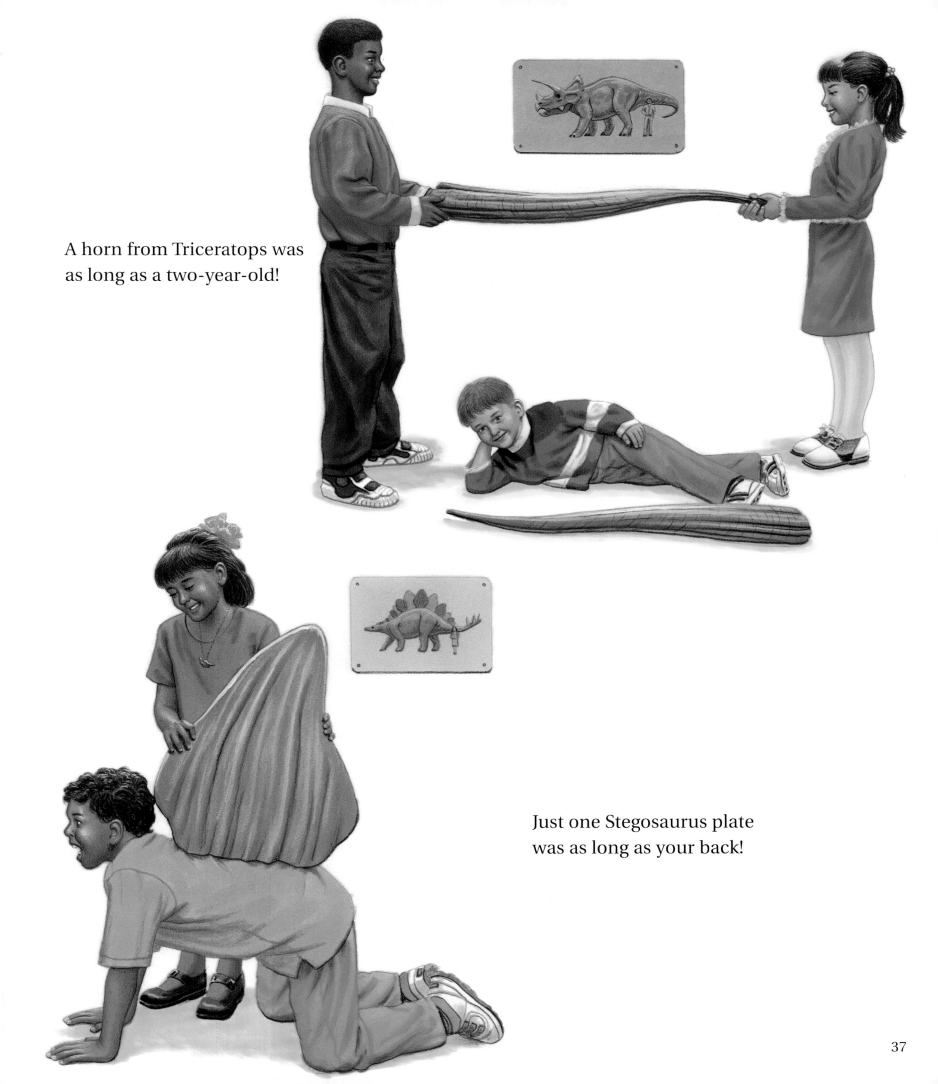

A horn from Triceratops was as long as a two-year-old!

Just one Stegosaurus plate was as long as your back!

GOOD-BYE, DINOSAURS

Dinosaurs lived on the earth for millions and millions of years. Then something happened that made them die out. The dinosaurs didn't die out all at once, though. It probably took many years. Maybe the weather changed, and the earth became too cold for dinosaurs. Or maybe something happened to kill the plants. The plant-eaters would have died out first. When there were no plant-eaters for the meat-eaters to eat, the meat-eaters would have died out. But no one knows for sure what happened.

Some day paleontologists may find fossils that tell us what happened to the dinosaurs. There are plenty of dinosaur bones left to find in the ground. Even though all the real dinosaurs are gone, there are still dinosaurs everywhere!